P9-DVO-686

An
Apple Pie
for Dinner

retold by **Susan VanHecke**

illustrated by **Carol Baicker-McKee**

Marshall Cavendish Children

The illustrations are rendered in bas-reliefs made from baked clay and mixed media.
Book design by Vera Soki
Editor: Margery Cuyler
Printed in China
First edition
1 3 5 6 4 2

mc Marshall Cavendish
Children

Library of Congress Cataloging-in-Publication Data
VanHecke, Susan.
   An apple pie for dinner / retold by Susan VanHecke; illustrated
by Carol Baicker-McKee.
     p. cm.
   Summary: Wishing to bake an apple pie, Old Granny Smith
sets out with a full basket, trading its contents for a series of
objects until she gets the apples she needs. Includes a recipe for
apple pie.
   ISBN 978-0-7614-5452-6
   [1. Barter—Fiction. 2. Neighborliness—Fiction. 3. Baking—
Fiction.] I. Baicker-McKee, Carol, 1958- ill. II. Title.
   PZ7.V3987App 2008   [E]—dc22
                   2008003664

For Dalton and Ava, the apples of my eye
—S.V.

For my mother, Teddy McKee,
with thanks for teaching me the satisfaction of sewing
and crafting, resourcefulness, and kindness
—C.B-M.

One day, old Granny Smith wanted
an apple pie for dinner.

She looked around her cozy kitchen.
She had flour and butter.
She had sugar and spices.
But there was one thing she didn't have.

She didn't have any apples.
Granny Smith had plums.
Lots of plums.
A tree full of purple plums.
But you can't make an apple pie from plums!

"I might find someone who has apples but needs plums," Granny thought.

So she filled a big basket with plums from her tree.

Then she put on her bonnet.

She pulled on her shawl.

And she set off.

Soon Granny met some chickens and a goose in the road.
"Cluck! Cluck! Honk! Honk!" the noisy birds squawked.
A young woman was feeding them.
"I have some plums," Granny said to the woman. "But I need some apples.
Do you have any apples?"
"Oh, my family likes plum jam best!" the woman said. "But all I have are
feathers. Will you take feathers for your plums?"

"Yes," said kind, old Granny, "if the plums will make your
family happy." And she traded her purple plums for a bag
of fluffy feathers.
"Thank you, thank you!" said the woman.
Granny smiled and continued on her way.

Soon Granny came to a beautiful garden, where she
heard a girl and a boy arguing.
"Cotton!" yelled the girl.
"Straw!" shouted the boy.
"May I help?" asked Granny.
"Mama is making a pillow. I think cotton is the
best stuffing. My brother thinks straw is best,"
said the girl.

"Feathers make the best stuffing," said Granny.
"They're softer than cotton and straw. Here."
Granny reached into her basket.
She gave the bag of fluffy feathers to the children.
"Thank you, thank you!" they said.
"I'm looking for apples," Granny said. "Do you have any?"

"We don't have any apples," said the two children.
"But here are some sweet-smelling flowers."

Granny smiled and continued on her way.

Soon Granny met a young prince dressed in his finest clothes.
He was going to see his ladylove, but he looked sad.
"May I help you?" asked Granny.
"I forgot the ring for my lady. It's too late to turn back, so I have
no gift for her," said the prince.

"Here's a gift for her," said Granny. She handed the prince the sweet-smelling flowers. "Thank you, thank you!" he said.
"I'm looking for apples," said Granny. "Do you have any?"

"I don't have apples," the prince said.
"But here's a gift for you." He gave
Granny a gold coin from his pocket.

Granny smiled and continued on her way.

Soon she came to a yard, where a mother and her children were crying.

"What's the matter?" Granny asked.

"We're hungry," sobbed the mother. "We have no money for food."

"Take this," said Granny. She gave the mother the gold coin. "Use it to buy food."
"Thank you, thank you!" the mother said.
"I'm looking for apples," Granny said. "Do you know where I might find some?"

"We don't have any apples," said the children.
"But we have pups that need good homes."
Granny put a small, brown dog in her basket.

She smiled and continued on her way.

Soon Granny came to a house, where she saw an old man sitting on a bench. He looked unhappy. "I'm lonely," he cried.

"You need a dog to keep you company," Granny said. She lifted the puppy from her basket.

"Woof-woof!" The puppy ran to the man and jumped in his lap.

"Thank you, thank you!" said the old man.

"I'm looking for apples," Granny said. "Do you have any?"

"Yes," said the old man, "I grow them
in my orchard." And he took her
to some apple trees.
"Thank you,
thank you!"
Granny said.

She filled her basket
with shiny apples.

Granny smiled and set off for home.

On her way, she invited everyone she had met to follow her.

In Granny's kitchen, they all worked together to bake a pie.

They peeled and sliced the apples.

They added some spices.

They rolled out the dough and filled the crust.

Then Granny popped the pie in the oven.

Soon, the pie was done. The crust was golden brown. The juices bubbled. The warm smell of cinnamon filled the kitchen.

Everyone sat down—and *yum yum*! What a delicious pie!
Granny looked around the table and smiled. "If you try
and try," Granny said to herself, "you can always have an
apple pie for dinner!"

And together, they ate every last crumb.

An apple pie for dinner

Would you like to make your own apple pie? Here's how—it's easy as pie!

To make your apple pie crust, you will need:

- 2 cups white flour
- 1 teaspoon salt
- 1 tablespoon granulated sugar
- 6 tablespoons softened butter
- 6 tablespoons shortening
- 4 tablespoons cold water

To make your dough:

In a large bowl, mix the flour, salt, and sugar. Add the butter and shortening and work with your fingers to make a mixture that looks like coarse meal. Add a few tablespoons of water one at a time so the mixture becomes stiff enough to pat into a ball. Sprinkle the ball with extra flour, wrap it in plastic wrap, and put it in the refrigerator for at least 20 minutes. With a grown-up's help, heat the oven to 400 degrees Fahrenheit.

To make your yummy apple pie filling, you will need:

- 6 Granny Smith apples (not purple plums, fluffy feathers, sweet-smelling flowers, a gold coin, or a small, brown dog!)
- 1/3 cup granulated sugar
- 1/3 cup brown sugar
- 2 tablespoons white flour
- 1/2 teaspoon ground cinnamon
- 1/2 teaspoon ground nutmeg
- 1/4 teaspoon salt
- 2 tablespoons butter, cut into small chunks

Ask a grown-up to help you peel, core, and slice your apples. Set aside. In a large bowl, blend the sugars, flour, cinnamon, nutmeg, and salt. Add your sliced apples to the bowl and mix until they are well coated.

Now put your pie together. Place your chilled dough on a cutting board that is lightly covered with flour. Ask a grown-up to help you cut the ball in half. With a rolling pin, roll out one half of the dough until it's shaped like a large, thin pancake. If the dough sticks to the rolling pin, add more flour. Set your "pancake" into a greased pie pan and press the dough to the bottom and sides. (The dough should overlap the rim.) Poke holes in the dough with a fork so steam can escape as the pie cooks.

Pour the coated apples into the pan. If there's any coating left over, sprinkle it on top of the apples. Scatter the butter chunks on top of the filling. You're almost done!

Roll out the rest of your dough. Set it on top of the apples so that its edge meets the edge of the bottom dough. Pinch the

edges of your dough together. Ask a grown-up to help you cut small slits in the top with a knife. This will let the steam escape.

Now it's time to bake! Ask a grown-up to put your pie in the oven. Set the timer for 50 minutes. Check your pie often. When the crust is golden and juice is bubbling through the slits, it's ready! Ask a grown-up to take it out. Let it cool for 1/2 hour.

Hooray! You did it. You just made your very own apple pie. Do you know the next step?

Yes! Eat every last crumb!

A Note from the Author

An Apple Pie for Dinner is based on an English folktale called "The Apple Dumpling." A dumpling is a ball of dough that is baked or boiled. Many years ago, a dumpling filled with fruit was a tasty treat. Today, an apple pie is a special treat. And it is extra yummy when helpful friends share it!

—S. V.

About the Illustrations

Carol Baicker-McKee created three-dimensional, mixed-media bas-reliefs to illustrate this book. Carol explains: "Mixed media is just a fancy way of saying that I created the artwork from lots of things, including fabric scraps sewn into clothing, embroidery, baked polymer clay, pipe cleaners, pieces of wood, and interesting things rescued from the trash and bought at rummage sales. Bas-relief is a technique in which the artwork—a combination of the above—is glued down on large pieces of foamcore. You can make your own mixed-media bas-relief pictures. Just use your imagination—and plenty of glue!"

Carol learned various crafts from her mother, Teddy McKee, who learned them from her mother, Frances Thorson. Besides being expert sewers, they baked, made hats, painted, and quilted.